Santa Claws

written by Laura Leuck ❧ illustrated by Gris Grimly

chronicle books · san francisco

COMFORT MATTRESSES

YOUR TICKET TO DEEP SLEEP

Here is what you need to do:

RENT-A-RAT

Fangs lost their bite?

Try **DENTU-FANG**

Call Doctor Drool, D.D.S., for an appointment.

KEEP THAT *emerald smile* SPARKLING WITH

GREEN GOO FANGPASTE

GREEN GOO FANG PASTE

Give your little monster hours of fun with the

BLACK MOON CLASSIC TITANIC and ICEBERG KIT

Die-cast Funeral **Hearse**

☞ DOORS OPEN
BLACK SATIN INTERIOR
COFFIN EXTRA

Add it to your collection today!

EAR WAX

FURNITURE POLISH

WILL MAKE YOUR COFFIN GLOW. A DROP-DEAD BARGAIN AT **$5.79**

EAR WAX FURNITURE POLISH

Make a statement with your pet.

MARGE'S VAMPIRE BATS

ALL SALES ARE FINAL.

NO BARKS! NO BITES!

ORDER YOUR PERFECT PET FROM

DEADFISH.COM

Teach your little warlock all he needs to know with

Witch Hazel's
25-PIECE POTION KIT

TRAP THE RAT
— ONLY —
$2.98
RAT NOT INCLUDED

PUT YOUR AD HERE!

CALL 7-1313-BADADS

To Susan Pearson, Editor Extraordinaire —L. L.
To all the naughty children —G. G.

Text © 2006 by Laura Leuck.
Illustrations © 2006 by Gris Grimly.
All rights reserved.

Book design by Sara Gillingham.
Typeset in Saturday Morning Toast, Monogram English and Windsor.
The illustrations in this book were rendered in watercolor and ink.
Manufactured in Hong Kong.

Library of Congress Cataloging-in-Publication Data
Leuck, Laura.
Santa Claws / written by Laura Leuck ; illustrated by Gris Grimly.
p. cm.
Summary: Rhyming text and illustrations follow the Christmas Eve activities
of monster boys Mack and Zack as they get ready for a visit from Santa Claws.
ISBN-13: 978-0-8118-4992-0 (alk. paper)
ISBN-10: 0-8118-4992-9 (alk. paper)
[1. Monsters—Fiction. 2. Santa Claus—Fiction. 3. Christmas—Fiction.
4. Stories in rhyme.]   I. Grimly, Gris, ill. II. Title.
PZ8.3.L565 Sa 2006
[E]—dc22
2005031582

Distributed in Canada by Raincoast Books
9050 Shaughnessy Street, Vancouver, British Columbia V6P 6E5

10 9 8 7 6 5 4 3 2 1

Chronicle Books LLC
85 Second Street, San Francisco, California 94105

www.chroniclekids.com

It's Christmas Eve in **Monster Town.**
The wind blows hard, the snow falls down.

It covers up a spooky shack
with broken bikes parked in the back.

Mack and Zack, two monster boys,
want gross and grisly Christmas toys—

MACK

ZACK

a potion kit,

a vampire bat,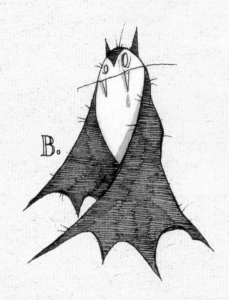

a hot new game called

Trap the Rat.

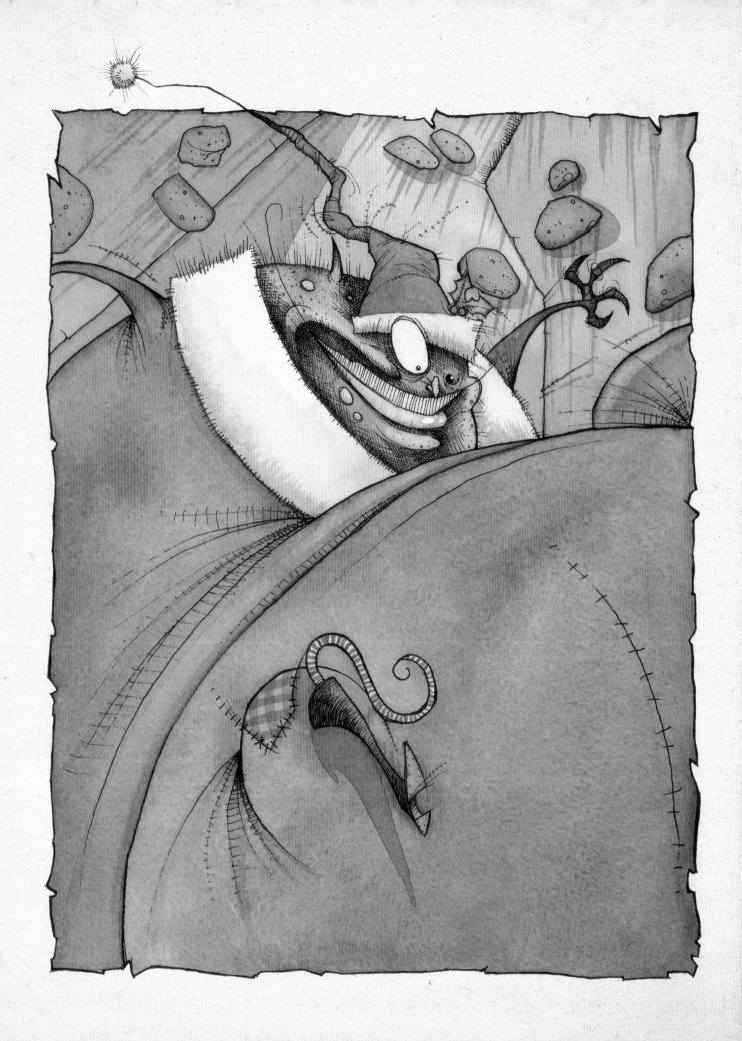

They've been so good the whole year through
so Santa will climb down their flue
with bulging sack and blood red suit,
a squirming snake tucked in his boot.

O Santa Claws, that fat old sprite
with pointy horns and teeth that bite,
who rides his dragon through the air,
bringing presents sure to scare.

They've hung it on the door, although
the boys are careful not to go
beneath the oozing blistertoe.

Their smelly socks are dripping dry
so Santa Claws won't pass them by.

They decorate their dead pine tree
and light the roof to help him see.
"Wreck the Halls" is loudly sung,
and on the front door, bones are hung.

They help make poisonberry pies,
crusty cookies topped with flies,
and eggnog mixed with spider feet,
in case ol' Claws should want a treat.

They brush their fangs, they scrub their paws
and comb their fur for Santa Claws,
then glancing at the darkened skies,
crawl into bed and close their eyes.

Snoring in their stinky beds,
boogerplums dance in their heads
while smoke of dragon fills the air.
Santa Claws will soon be there!

And when the morning lights come on
Santa's slimy snacks are gone!
Toys surround their withered tree—
Seven...fifteen...twenty-three!

So do what little monsters should—
try your hardest to be good,
and you will find that if you do . . .

Santa Claws may visit **you**!